The Millennium Gene

The Facts and The Fiction

Sam Martin

The Millennium Gene

British Library Cataloguing-in-publication data
A catalogue record for this book is available from the British Library.
Copyright ©2001 by Sam Martin
Published by The Writers Cooperative, 6 Chaplin Grove, Crownhill,
Milton Keynes. Bucks. MK8 0DQ
Email: writers@beamish3.fsnet.co.uk

ISBN   1-902651-42-1

First Edition 2001

CONTENTS

Forward by Professor Fred Brown, OBE FRS.

The Gene Age

Betsy- The Gorp

I should have waited

Love

My Lucky gene

Johnny's Decision

Hunting genes

Ferromites

Superbug

Adventures in Viroland

A New Pair of Genes

Foreword

Our understanding of genetics, especially at the molecular level, has progressed during the last 20 years in an explosive fashion, far beyond the expectations of the scientists who in the early seventies devised novel strategies that permitted the swapping and switching of genes among organisms and across species. Like all major scientific discoveries and techniques, genetic engineering and the new reproductive technologies have unfolded details in the fundamentals of genetics and given a depth of understanding of living systems undreamt of a few years ago. A new industry, biotechnology, has emerged which depends on the manipulation of genes of plants, animals, and humans, providing exciting ways of increasing the quality and quantity of food and of treating diseases. Spectacular announcements are made almost daily about new 'gene' discoveries and even more spectacular predictions are made about their impact and potential dangers.

Like much of genetic engineering, Sam Martin's book, *The Millennium Gene,* is a hybrid. The initial chapter provides a factual survey of the current situation showing where major advances will have an impact in the not too distant future. This is followed by a series of short fictional stories based on a selection of scenarios, which illustrate the possible impact of some current advances especially in the medical field, but also of importance in agriculture and the environment.

Developing from a course of Ethics, which he gave at Queen's University, Belfast, Sam Martin has produced a useful book which should stimulate discussion about these important issues. Each theme has a realistic scientific basis which is woven into a variety of human situations in sensitive, captivating and sometimes humorous ways illustrating the ethical, moral, safety and monetary aspects. A useful addendum to the stories is an up dating of his Inaugural lecture 'A New Pair of Genes' given at Queen's University in 1981 which includes a brief outline of the history of genetics, molecular biology and gene cloning strategies. This should be useful for readers who are not familiar with this area of science.

Throughout the book, there are also serious messages for scientists, industrialists, the public, and governments. Each must be responsible, not only for the past but also for the future. Scientists must be aware of more than the last experimental result or publication; industrialists, for more than the figures at the bottom of the balance sheet; the general public must be able to look beyond their immediate fears and accept the realities of risk, for the sake of a better future; and governments, world-wide, must endeavour to develop codes of practice and regulations that provide confidence and respect both within their nations and across their across borders. There are advantages for everyone if the issues are discussed in a calm atmosphere.

I have known Sam Martin as a scientific colleague and close friend for almost forty years. He has always been interested in the impact of science on the environment and perhaps more important, on the human spirit. This interest shines through very clearly in this little book

Fred Brown, OBE, PhD, HonDSc (QUB), FRS. **July 2000**

The Gene Age

Few, if any, can now have failed to have seen the double helical image of DNA or have heard of the recent developments in genetic engineering, biotechnology and the new reproductive technologies, such as *in vitro* fertilisation, xenotransplantation and cloning. In the eyes of the public all have become merged under the GM banner and the Human Genome Project, now nearing the completion of the first phase, seen as a major icon of the new millennium. One face of the icon gives us great hope for the future based on our better understanding, control, and beneficial exploitation of the genes of animal, plants, and man. The other face causes us great concern. How will this information be abused? How can we control and prevent mistakes from happening? To many people the concept of our genes have become sacred, rather like the concept of our soul and of course this begs the question of how can we dare change them.

Of course, we hear a lot about the potential benefits of the new technologies, of better medicines, vaccines and drugs, of cheaper food and longer life. We hear a lot about the dangers and ethics of these new Frankenstein technologies, of hazards to the wild life and environment, the fear of new diseases and a new eugenics. However, we hear little of the complex and sophisticated regulatory bodies that control and govern everything that is done in the scientific field of GM research. These bodies have and are establishing a legal framework for future development and exploitation of biotechnology and one of their major objectives for the next millennium is to create confidence and awareness in the general public that at present does not seem to exist. To this end, I will describe a few genetic scenarios that will illustrate questions that will concern us all in the next millennium.

Firstly is the possibility of screening for defective genes. This technology was developed in order to help people who were likely to carry the genes responsible for certain inherited diseases such as cystic fibrosis or of our susceptibility to certain diseases such as cancer, high blood pressure or Alzheimer's disease. However, it is not surprising that the financial implications of this latent knowledge has come to be of interest to insurance companies, banks and employers and it seems inevitable that there will be a continuing demand to involve comprehensive genetic information in the process of financial decision making. In the longer term, as more information accumulates it is also possible that gene screening will also be involved in educational prediction and career development. Some may find this approach beneficial and economically desirable while others feel it an assault on their freedom.

The second issue that is currently undergoing a great debate is the possibility that animals may be genetically modified in such a way that their organs can be used for human transplantation without the risk of rejection. This is generally known as xenotransplantation. There is presently a real dilemma here. Firstly, the technique seems to work and if widely available would greatly reduce the long waiting list for transplantation, especially for kidney and heart transplants. However, it is still unclear whether there would be risk of a latent virus/agent, in for example the pig, becoming a pathogen in the human. We know that the technology involved could permit cross species barriers to be broken down as may have happened with BSE and CJD. However, should such hazards be overcome, are there any real ethical problems about the transplantation of animal organs? After all, we have used animal organs and products for food and medicine for many thousands of years.

A third topic that has caused great excitement during the last few decades is that of developments in reproductive technologies. These have at least matched those in the field of genetic engineering and unfortunately have now become almost synonymous with it, at least in the minds of the general public. Within a few years, we have gone from artificial insemination, through to *in vitro* fertilisation and genetic screening of embryos and to direct cloning from adult tissue. Added to the emerging abilities to screen comprehensively for specific genes, defective or otherwise, ensures that the future of reproductive biologies is very much on the ethical agenda. Within weeks of the first successful cloning of a sheep, Dolly, we have seen the question of human cloning jump to the top of the biological charts. Right or wrong, certain people want to and will try to clone humans. Of course the agricultural community will lead the way and with every economic and health and safety justification the children of the next millennium will eat cloned meat. However, will they have cloned brothers and sisters and school friends?

Whereas in the agricultural sphere the novel reproductive technologies have been developed for economic reasons, in the human context they have been actively pursued in order to help overcome medical and health problems associated with either inherited diseases or infertility. These are all noble causes and I feel sure that few would want it any other way. Nevertheless, as we have seen with the ability to screen for defective genes, other pressing financial concerns immediately bear upon these new technologies. What circumstances could justify the cloning of humans? What financial and social pressures would make this become a viable and acceptable option?

However, first we must eliminate the irrational and historic fear about cloning, based mainly on science fiction stories. We may eventually have thousands of identical pigs, sheep and cows on our farms, just as we already have thousands of identical trees and plants and flowers all around us, but I see no real justification for cloning thousands of copies of anyone, alive or dead. The ability of cloning from adult tissue, should indeed it prove to be feasible with humans and that has not yet been shown, has completely changed the face of even the science fiction scenarios. There would be absolutely no need to clone multiple copies of anyone, when everyone could have one or perhaps a few copies of themselves. Even in one of the worst doomsday scenarios of universal male infertility, because of the environmental pollution of water supplies by excess oestrogen or an unforeseen worldwide catastrophe, the demand to repopulate the earth would not be now dependent upon some single clone. Fortunately, to day we are not yet living in the world of science fiction or with an imminent doomsday scenario, but in the real world where these issues will not hopefully have to be faced. Rather these new techniques should be developed and exploited in a mature and responsible way. Nonetheless the rate of development of the new genetics is currently so rapid and in general the social concerns so great, that it is difficult to predict just how far into the next millennium it will be, before the practice and products of the GM revolution will become widely acceptable. Hopefully we shall experience their benefits, as many have already done in the medical field, and come to appreciate and have confidence in the regulatory controls that govern the development and use of all GM-related work.

As we start the new millennium and the words GM food are on the lips of us all, it is worth recalling that this so-called new technology of genetic manipulation or as originally called recombinant DNA, was first developed over twenty five years ago, in the early 1970's. In fact, around 1975, scientists from across the world self-imposed a moratorium on GM research until the safety aspects could be better understood. Now official regulatory bodies and committees control what and how experiments are done. The sudden appearance on shop shelves of GM food, especially in the UK, has produced an unexpected, if belated, negative reaction from a health conscious public. No doubt, previous mistakes made by the agricultural industry, most likely, resulting in the BSE crisis, has magnified greatly the fears about the new GM foods, and it is right that the industry is asked to look again at the unresolved aspects of safety and environmental impact. However, in the public's ultimate decision about the acceptability of GM foods or drugs or vaccines, it is vitally important to untangle the concerns over physically related issues such as safety and environmental impacts and the personal beliefs about the rightness or wrongness of switching genes between organisms by means that are said to be 'unnatural'. Such an approach will be a return to medieval philosophies and will hold up the development of the life sciences, as was the case in the Middle Ages when we were told to believe that the earth was flat and was in the centre of the universe! However, hopefully as we enter the new millennium we are at the beginning of a new adventure in our understanding of Life and inspire of scares and fears and worries and rumour, we will ultimately benefit from this new knowledge. Finally, the most exciting development in the new millennium will be the completion of the first phase of the Human Genome Project, when the complete list of human genes will become available. The next phase will provide real functional information, about what the 100,000 genes, that are present in each of our cells, actually do. The large majority of these may have very little to do with what we may think of as a disease or illness and are probably involved with behavioural, character and physical traits or abilities such as social, artistic, physical or other skills. Indeed, the human genome project will open up an unread book of our genetic make up, which together with the new and improving cloning and reproductive technologies, will provide the Human Race with much discussion and debate over the next millennium.

BETSY- The GORP

We collected Betsy from the clinic the day after my retirement dinner. It had been a nice affair and my many years of service to the Company had been gratefully acknowledged. The Managing Director himself, whom we all affectionately knew as the Chief, had presented me with the traditional clock which would allow Helen and me to watch the years slip by, as indeed it has. Of course, the staff had also made a collection and I had been well liked and there had been sufficient funds for Helen and me to buy Betsy. At that time, Betsies had become very popular retirements gifts.

Helen had brought along a lovely hand knitted woollen blanket that had been used for Sarah our little daughter when she was a baby. Unfortunately, Sarah and Jack, her husband, had provided us with no grandchildren, as like so many of their generation they were infertile but they both had successful careers and they didn't seem to have time for children anyway. For us, a Betsy would have to do just fine.

"Now, don't overfeed her," the nurse at the clinic warned as she handed over Betsy and Helen wrapped the tiny bundle of pinkness into the white woolly blanket. "Continue to let her have one bottle of milk three times a day, then by the end of the week begin to transfer her on to solids. She'll be well weaned by the end of the month."

"My goodness!" Helen said excitedly, rubbing Betsy's damp pink nose with the knuckle of her forefinger, "she will be growing quickly then."

"Oh yes," the nurse said, as she left us at the entrance, "they grow very quickly, but don't forget to come back for her booster vaccinations and a check in three months."

I drove the car back home, always looking sideways, trying to catch a glimpse of the pink bundle and the little eyes that I could feel looking at me with curiosity. "She'll stay in tonight, won't she?" I asked, a little pleading in my voice, knowing that Helen had never been keen on an animal in the house.

"Of course," Helen said, reconciled to the idea from the moment she had taken Betsy from the nurse. "You couldn't put this little angel out just yet. We couldn't risk her getting a chill."

As the nurse had warned, Betsy grew quickly and was never satisfied. She would have taken three bottles at a time rather than one and gulped it all without stopping once she got the teat into her snout. Of course, it wasn't really a snout to us. Her soft gentle pink lips and moist shiny nose that loved poking into every crevice it could find was the part of Betsy that we came to love the most in those early childhood days. Betsy's fine pink skin was soon covered with a silky silver down that was beautiful to stroke and she often lay in my lap in the evening, her chin resting on the arm of the chair watching the movements on the television. And the nurse was right about the solids. By the end of the week, things in the kitchen were beginning to disappear. Anything that accidentally dropped was immediately devoured. Bottles were discarded by the end of the week and bright new dishes of milk and meal were soon prominent features of our kitchen floor.

Betsy liked the garden, especially the plants and shrubs that I'd spent most of my life nurturing and tending so that they'd be nice to look at during my well-deserved retirement. Now I spent a lot of time protecting my special botanical creations with wire netting and defences of various sorts in an attempt to keep Betsy's gnawing teeth from attacking everything above ground, let alone underground, which she loved doing at the slightest smell of a mouse or a mole or even a worm. Fortunately we had a large garden and I soon had it divided into special areas were Betsy could roam and play unrestricted. We had been told to give her plenty of exercise and not to let her get frustrated, otherwise the whole Gorping experiment would be wasted.

It was nice being retired. Helen and I walked Betsy every morning and evening around the local park. At first people looked at her with some surprise and dogs in general showed, a lot of early interest, but Betsy treated these lower animals with the disdain that they deserved. Soon she stood head and shoulders above and was a good many pounds weightier than the largest of the local fauna and she had gained their respect. Her coat had matured into a silver mantle of long fine hair that dropped from the centre of her back down each side until it was nearly but not quite touching the ground. Strangers often asked us if it was a new breed of dog, but when we said, "No, she's a Gorp," they looked at us with surprise or horror, I never knew which, and walked on.

Of course, at the time I retired, all those years ago, few people knew much about Gorps. Like most people, neither Helen nor I had ever thought much about the modern technologies and we'd never thought that some day we would actually own a Gorp. However, we well remember the TV programme many years ago that introduced us to the concept of Gorpping and really got us started.

As you know, nowadays it has become very popular and in the evenings, the Park is full of Gorps. I remember when we got our third Gorp, Betsy III, we started a local Gorp Club, and have recently negotiated the purchase of the local, unused, school sports field so that we have more room to exercise them. We've won prizes at the National Gorp Show and in fact, the money we won ten years ago year helped Helen get her own Gorp. As you know, at our age, it is best not to risk it with just one, but we always remember Betsy I, with the most affection.

Looking back it was probably one of the saddest days in our life when we had to use Betsy. She had become like a second daughter to us. She was so very intelligent. She watched television when other animals were on the screen and wagged her curly tail, her tiny black eyes looking up with delight, nuzzling into my pocket to steal my hanky, waiting for that special tit-bit, patiently, while I was having supper, loyal, loving, devoted Betsy. Helen and I cried when she had to go. Anyway, our Betsies have been a great success. Pity we haven't any grandchildren, but then we've loved our Gorps. We still walk them twice every day and they get brushed and groomed most afternoons. They look so beautiful with all that long silky silver hair.

Some people didn't like us keeping Gorps, but then we've lived the longest and we don't want to see our Betsies kept in unhygenic cages and pens in factory farms. I'm sure they wouldn't be half as healthy. They'd have become infected with all sorts of things, if we didn't care for them like we do. Look what happened to Sarah and Jack. They were too busy to look after children let alone a Gorp. Then Jack got into trouble and he asked Helen to give him her Betsy. But of course, she couldn't do that. After a long wait, Jack had got one of the government Gorps and he hasn't been right since. They say he's got an antibiotic resistant infection. In fact, he's very ill. We feel awful about it. We really should have let them have one of our Gorps but then Helen and I were due to be gorpped again in a couple of months. How were we to know? Still we feel awful, although Sarah says, it's not our fault.

Of course, Helen and I had been over fifty when Gorpping had first become available and we were really very lucky to have had it done just in time. It was clear that my heart wouldn't last me much beyond seventy and Helen's kidneys were already on the blink, so the chance of getting a tailor made Gorp seemed very sensible and especially if by keeping it yourself, you reduced the costs and the waiting lists substantially. In fact, with our meagre medical insurance we couldn't afford it any other way. I've had three heart transplants and Helen has had her kidneys done twice. They've lasted about ten years each, so time's going along nicely and we've had great health all these years.

But now the Government are saying that there has to be a limit to the number of Gorp transplants we'll be allowed in future. It's become too expensive. I can remember the time when the Government paid half the costs of our first Gorp, Betsy I, as the Company donated the rest as part of my retirement present. Well I suppose we can't expect things to last forever, but Helen and I will keep going as long as we can. In the meantime, it's time for our Betsies' walk. They're standing looking dejected, grunting at us.

22

"I should have waited"

Was she right to be coming back? Laura wondered as
we had dozed in our comfortable seats in Concorde on our way
over from New York.

Now I was only sorry that we'd got separated from
Harry. He'd just been so slow at the steps that Laura, mother
and I had moved on ahead. He took ages. Everyone else had
settled, and there was that embarrassed silence, except for the

persistent tap of his stick on the wooden floor as Harry made his slow progression down to the front pew. He'd resisted Sally's offer to help him put his stick into the umbrella rack, and eventually had to hook it over the back of the pew, mumbling an apology to Uncle Tom.

A tear came to my eye as Dad's coffin was carried down the aisle. We all knew it was a relief, especially to Mum, who was worn out by the strain of caring for him these long years. The words of 'Abide with me' came back as the organ music and the voices of the congregation filled the church, but I could not read the hymn sheet. It had been happening more often over the past few months but I had always tried to ignore it, always making some excuse to myself. Now the shake in my hand had become so obvious that Laura had to share her hymn sheet with me.

The Rev Thomas prayed and reflected on father's life. Dad had been a very successful rugby player and mountaineer when young and had done well in his job. However, he had ignored his growing problem, successfully hiding it from others, even Mum, for a long time until it suddenly caught up with him and then everything had collapsed. There was no cure for MLPP. Just a long slow mid-life progressive paralysis that eventually reduced him to a helpless shell. But his mind remained clear and alert and his strength of character shone through his agony until near the end.

By the last hymn, Laura was getting tired and I saw her hand spread unconsciously over her swollen belly. I squeezed her hand and prayed that everything would be all right. We had agreed to join the clinical trial for the new gene therapy procedures on human embryos for certain conditions such as MLPP.

After the cremation, we returned to the family home that was old and musty. In the lounge, the heavy dusty violet curtains were still half drawn, and in the shady corner, Aunt Maud poured tea.

Harry had slumped in Dad's old armchair on the left hand side of the fireplace. "You just look like your father," Mum said unwittingly as Sally gave him his midday tablets and helped him with a cup of tea.

"I know. I've got his dammed genes," snapped Harry, pushing the offered teacup away and swallowing his medication with a grimace.

"You don't need to take it out on Sally," I snapped. "She's been very good to you." I'd been horrified at Harry's attitude, which had changed so much since I'd seen him about six years ago.

"It's the drugs," Sally offered, shielding Harry from my scorn. "They're upsetting him." She kissed him on the forehead.

"Sorry my dear, you're the only one that understands me," he smiled at her and you could see in their eyes that love still lingered on, even if only by a thread.

"So you're going to have a baby," Aunt Maud said to Laura. "When is it due? You look as though it might arrive any minute."

"He's to be induced in two weeks," Laura said. "The baby's doing well."

"Never thought you'd have had a baby after all these years," Uncle Tom said through a mouthful of cake, "especially knowing about Ian's father and poor Harry there."

"We thought a lot about that, Uncle Tom," I said, defending our position. "After all, the defective gene that is responsible for MLPP has been known for many years. Now they can inject the corrected gene into embryonic cells following in vitro fertilisation. Then when the embryos are a few days old and have been checked to ensure that they contain the corrected gene, they are implanted. If the correct gene is present during early development of the baby the person will never take the disease."

"I don't understand it at all," Mum said, sitting down beside Laura. "Father wouldn't have approved, you know. But of course, I do hope and pray that you'll be all right. Both of you."

"I think you're wrong," Harry said from the depths of his leather armchair. "You shouldn't have let them talk you into getting involved with that sort of thing. What if the experiment doesn't work and the infant turns out like me?"

"Indeed, Harry," Uncle Tom mumbled through a second slice of cake, "I don't believe in experiments on people. Sounds a bit like what Hitler did."

"It would have been immoral in my day," Aunt Maud said, not wanting to insult anyone present, but not able to withhold her indignation that something unholy was going on in front of her very eyes.

"Aunt Maud's right," Harry responded, aggressively. "It's immoral. I suppose if the embryo hadn't been OK, it would have been aborted. Is that not what you'd agreed to?" He didn't wait for an answer. He was on a high and there was to be no stopping him now.

However, Uncle Tom had finished his cake and the blatant immorality of what was going on in their very midst had stirred his religious fervour. "I agree with you Harry," he

28

always had, "look at your father, my own brother, William. What would have happened to him if they'd found he had that bad gene before he'd been born? Aborted him nowadays, most likely. Just, look at the good life he had. Brought you two into the world and there's your mother. Do you regret his life, Sadie?"

"Not for a second." Mum looked across at me, tears brimming in her eyes. "Your Dad was a wonderful man, Ian, despite his illness. I just hope that this wee one will be as good." She kissed Laura on the cheek.

Harry had become even more morose. "I suppose the next step after abortion is euthanasia," he murmured just loud enough for us to hear. "I suppose you really want to get rid of me, too. Couldn't even wait for me to get down the church this morning at my own father's funeral. Wishing I'd been in the coffin beside him. He's a useless vegetable, wasting Sally's life, that's what you're all thinking. Well, Ian, my young brother, you just wait. I can see it coming, if you can't."

"Someone has to take the initiative," I responded, annoyed again at Harry's negative attitude. "Progress will never be made if people don't take risks. They needed volunteers and it was logical for us to join the trial. Surely, the important thing is that our MLPP gene will be eliminated forever. Our son will be able to have children without the fear of passing on this horrible condition that Dad has just died from and Harry has and yes, Harry, damn it, I have it too. See!" I remember holding out my trembling hand towards him and he took it and pressed it, momentarily, tears in his eyes, and then pushed it away and ignoring my comments, ranted on, turning his venom on Laura in a way that shocked everyone in the room.

"You think you're clever. Get your name in the newspaper, I suppose. Make a fortune by writing your story for some Sunday Rag. However, have you thought about whether or not it should be done at all? Where will it lead too? Who will decide what is good and what is bad? Who is to be kept and who is to be eliminated? We all have to learn to live with the good and the bad in us. That's God's will and we shouldn't interfere with it."

Suddenly I realised that Laura was in pain. Her head was thrown back on the settee and her face grimaced in agony. "Damn you, Harry! Just leave me alone." She screamed again as the cramps returned, "God, the baby's coming!" and before we could reach her she rolled off the settee onto the floor.

I've cursed myself ever since. I knew we should have waited for Harry at the Church steps. It had been my entire fault. Our son was born that afternoon upstairs on Dad's old bed. Tragically, Laura died during the birth without ever seeing her beautiful little son, William, whom she had wanted so much.

But, William has grown up to be a fine man and is married himself now and they've just had a son. They've called him, Ian, after me. Of course, the MLPP gene has been successfully eliminated, thank goodness. It was thanks to Laura, really. She showed the way, but how I've missed her all these years. Harry had been lucky that he'd had Sally to look after him. It's been lonely in this Home, and the drugs make me sleep and dream a lot and I keep remembering how I should have waited for Harry at the church and Laura wondering, 'was she right to be coming back?' My grandson, Ian, is coming tomorrow and I'm looking forward to that!

LOVE

Love to Gerry and me had meant more than just ourselves. We'd wanted a family. Always had and tried very hard for years but like everyone else having a baby had become rare and is now practically unheard off. The Doctors tell us that things are going to be all right again.

Nowadays, when you looked around the village, most of the youngsters have been adopted from abroad and there are no very young children. About ten years ago one of our very wealthy neighbours, in the big house at the top of the hill, had managed to adopt a child after a long search spending a lot of time and money. Cynthia Ramsay, she's very nice, really, though her husband is a real snob, had all of us up from the village for afternoon tea to see their new baby. He was a lovely little black bundle and I could have kept him myself. I could hardly give him back to Cynthia who passed him round everyone for a brief cuddle.

The sight and the feel of the little orphan had got us all remembering and talking about what had happened out there. When you learn things in school about history it always seems ages ago, but really this has all happened within our lifetime. I first heard of AIDS at school when there was all the talk about safe sex and things. Dad used to say that when he was young, contraceptives were used to stop folk having babies, then suddenly they were being used to stop you getting disease. Of course, the AIDS scare didn't affect us very much really, because Gerry and I had been in love since we'd first met at school and have never been with anyone else. I suppose it's one of the advantages of living in a small community where everyone knows everyone else and sleeping around as it were was certainly frowned upon, and of course the Priest then kept a close eye on our ongoing activities and friendships and wasn't a bit afraid of speaking frankly during a Sunday morning mass or confession.

Of course, early in the new millennium the great news was that an AIDS vaccine had been made. Suddenly we were all to be safe. I remember my old Dad saying shortly before he died that it was just like what happened with polio. One day it was there and next day it had gone. Swimming pools were opened again and within a year, everyone had forgotten about it. AIDS would have been the same. A great slump in the contraceptive market was expected and a predicted increases in the number of illegitimate babies.

Of course, it wasn't to be. No one could have predicted the outpouring of Roaring Syphilis from the ravages of Rwanda that spread across the world at an astonishing rate. Once in the international travel network there was no stopping it. You didn't need to have sex, even going to the loo while travelling, was a death trap. Before the world really knew, what was going on RS was all over the place. Completely antibiotic resistant and transmitted by stable airborne spores, Roaring Syphilis became the most common major disease throughout the world.

Gerry must have picked it up on the way back from Delhi during one of his many business trips. He was one of the first Europeans to catch RS and it took the doctors quite a while to decide what he had. I couldn't believe it at first and he swore that he'd never been unfaithful. I nearly left him over it, but that was a long time ago and I'm just now so relieved that we're both as well as can be expected. We were very lucky and it didn't affect us too badly. Gerry got the fever and then a week later I got it and the roaring genital lesions that so were very itchy. We got better eventually but the doctors told us that we'd most likely be infertile and should count ourselves lucky that we'd only got a relatively mild dose

Unfortunately, most people in the village got RS too and blamed Gerry for bring it in. Of course, it was sheer coincidence that we'd had a party for our tenth wedding anniversary a few days after day after Gerry came back from that trip and most of our neighbours in the village were there. We all thought that poor Gerry had just gone down with a dose of 'flu that evening. Nevertheless, of course the whole village was itching like hell by the end of the month and sadly, there's hardly been a baby born since.

Now after all these years I can't really believe when I feel the movements in my tummy. They're actually kicking. It won't be long now and I'm told that they're going to be just like Gerry. The next pair we have will be mine.

It took a long time for the Government to decide to legalise cloning, but this was the only thing to do to solve the infertility crisis. I don't really think The Roaring Syphilis was all that bad, as if you were healthy, your own immunity cleared it up eventually, like it did with most of us, and RS probably wasn't the only cause for infertility. We all knew for years, before we ever heard of Roaring Syphilis, that many people, including ourselves, were having difficulty getting babies and there was a lot of talk even then about the effects of the Pill and hormone derivatives and related toxic chemicals in the water sources that were making men infertile. Many scientists said so, although the Governments never admitted it. They found it convenient to blame poor Africa. However, the Old Roaring Syphilis put the nail in the coffin, as it were, and gave governments the excuse they needed to legalise cloning.

There's no going back now and if we want to have another generation of children then we just have to clone. I think we're damn lucky that we know how too. Of course, farmers have been cloning animal for years, ever since the famous Dolly experiment on the sheep. I remember drawing a picture of Dolly when in primary school which got a prize at the end of the year. Never thought for a moment that I'd be the first in the village to have my husband's cloned twins.

Father John was in the other day and gave us his blessing. He hadn't liked the idea at all at first when Gerry and I had told him what we wanted to do. Of course, they'd been cloning in England for some years and the American children are nearly all cloned now. Some people say that the Chinese always have been, but I know that's just supposed to be a joke. To me a busload of Chinese tourists always look alike and I could well believe that they had been cloned, but I know that's just nonsense. We had a coach load of young American tourists through the village last week and they were all different, just like you and me. There were two identical sisters, but they were dressed differently and just looked like any ordinary pair of twins. I just can't imagine anyone wanting to make a whole busload of identical twins. Not unless they wanted to put them in a circus or something. Perhaps a trapeze troop would benefit, but I can't imagine even a football team made up of eleven Georgie Bests.

No, we're just having the two. The doctors advised that at my age I would be better to have twins if we want to get a family started, also I think they may have been concerned that one may not have done. Anyway, I glad both are doing well and we're really looking forward to having the two of them. Father John mentioned it at Mass and helped to change a lot of people's attitudes in the village. In fact, over the last few months, quite a number of villagers have either had the treatment or are on the waiting list. There's going to be a lot of babies in the village over the next few years. Just as well, mind you, for what on earth would we have done as we get older and there are no young people around? I remember Mum and Dad when they were ill. What would they have done if we hadn't been here to look after them? May be in a big city you can get outside help, but in a small isolated village like ours there is no one but the family and a few close friends. If we didn't start new babies now in twenty years time the whole place would be empty. Of course, I don't want you to think that we just want children so that they can grow up to look after us. That's not true at all. That's what worried Father John at the start, but I just said to him, 'if the farmers can clone animals for food, surely we can clone babies for Love.'

My Lucky Gene

If I'd known what was going to happen I'd never have bothered filling in the little form at the back of the Sunday World and sending it off in response to that 'Guaranteed for Life' advertisement. It wasn't a very big form. Just a few details about date of birth and our family history and any illness or diseases that we'd suffered. They also asked for a small sample of hair, just a few strands, pulled-out by the roots.

That was the most difficult part in fact. Getting a few nice strands of hair with roots intact was more difficult than I'd thought and Selene and I pulled and tugged at each other's hair for some time before being satisfied that we'd got good samples. After all, we wouldn't want them to reject us just because of a poor piece of hair.

We didn't hear anything for about a month and had nearly forgotten all about the advert that we'd spent that rainy Sunday afternoon playing around with. We were rushing out to work one morning when the big glossy envelope arrived through the post with the bold heading 'Guaranteed for Life' embossed on the top left hand corner.

"That's that advert thing," Selene said, dumping the envelope on the coffee table and gathering up her homework papers and books that she'd been marking late into the previous night.

I gave it a mere glance but kept thinking about it all day as I patrolled the superstore on the lookout for shop lifters and delinquents. It was a quiet day and there had only been one minor incident when a woman who was a well-known kleptomaniac tried to walk out wearing an expensive fur coat. We all knew Betty. It was a game to her really, and she couldn't help herself. She was around the Store nearly every day. The police knew her well and she'd been in hospital a number of times, but they said it was all in her genes and there was really nothing they could do, except keep her on the pills.

Anyway, the likes of Betty kept me in a job and it was better than working in the quarry on the edge of the town.

The image of the big glossy envelope kept coming back to me all through the day. I didn't normally get big envelopes and kept wondering what it would say. Most likely, they'd give us a chance to win a prize by filling in another questionnaire. However, I did hope they'd offer us a good pension rate. We were both healthy and it would be good to get our pension arrangements sorted out when we were still fairly young. Of course, we should have done it sooner, after we'd got married but then we'd other things to do and buy and I always hoped to get a good job with a pension. Unfortunately, unemployment had become worse over the last few years and I'd just managed to keep going by taking anything I could get. We were very lucky that Selene had her part time teaching post, but that didn't have a pension linked to it either so we had been attracted by the advert.

I was home first, and opened a can of beer and the big envelope. There were three files inside; one was for Selene, another for us both and the third for me. I put the others aside and neatly opened mine down the edge. The covering letter thanked me for my application and hoped that I would take the opportunity of joining their pension scheme. There were projections of what I would pay each month and what I would get at various ages whenever I decided to retire. I could retire at any time over 45 years of age and my pension would be guaranteed for life. Unfortunately, it did not seen very much, if fact there was no way I could imagine living on that! I leafed over the other sheets of glossy expensive paper, which outlined in more detail the basis of their proposal. By the time Selene came in, ladened as usual with books and homeworks, I was in a flaming temper.

"Have you not got the dinner made yet?" Selene moaned as she threw her bag down on the settee, "You knew I'd be late."

"Oh sorry, it's this damned pension thing. You should see what they offer me and worse than that, they say I've got a lot of bad genes that they can't insure."

We had a rushed cold tea and then got down to comparing our letters in detail. Selene kept saying that she'd have to get on with her marking but the dossiers were very comprehensive and the more we read the more angry and worried we became. Apparently, by signing and returning the form at the bottom of the small advert, we had given them permission to do a complete scan of our DNA using the small sample of hair, and from the store of information about human genes in their huge computer data bank they were able to assess a fantastic number of our characteristics and defects. They said that this information was provided free, and that their offer of a pension was the best offer that under the circumstances could possibly be made. The back pages of the dossier contained a long and comprehensive list of diseases and conditions and the computer had blacked out a small square beside a considerable number of them. Each of these conditions were given a numerical factor, which we noticed were different for men and women, and on the final page of the dossier there was a computation of all these factors resulting in a calculation of the final value of the proposed pension.

We eagerly traced down the list, comparing each others predisposition to Alzheimer's Disease, breast cancer, bladder cancer, heart disease, lung disease, kidney disease, liver disease, MS, ovarian cancer, schizophrenia, it went on and on. There seemed to be few conditions that at least one of us was not threatened with even if only at a low risk. Selene was threatened with having breast cancer, ovarian cancer and MS while I was nearly sure to have a heart attack and develop Alzheimer's. The basic pension took all these risks into account but for extra premiums, they would give us special cover for these high-risk conditions. It was all very sensible if you could afford it.

A third file, which had fallen on the floor under the coffee table, was addressed to both of us, and had a warning notice printed clearly across the front, saying that we should not read this dossier unless we wished to know about the possible gene profiles of our children. We were beginning to think of starting a family although at present we couldn't afford to and any thought of having sex just then had been completely squashed by reading the dossiers. Selene tore open the file and pulled out the glossy sheets of the third dossier. There was a glossy colour computerised photo-image of our most probable child. It would have red hair, and blue eyes and, like me, a disfiguring hair-lip. The computer printout went on to say that we were strongly advised not to have children, as the predicted gene profiles would make it difficult for them to obtain insurance cover.

We went to bed that night, despondent and humiliated. Selene wept, suddenly realising just how much she wanted a baby. Of course, my father had had Alzheimer's and Selene's mother had died from breast cancer, but they had lived a good happy life for over 60 years and I can't say I haven't enjoyed my life and Selene loves me, hair-lip and all. Why have we become so possessed with our genes and what is going to happen, when all we want is to enjoy life as best we can and love each other and our family for as long as we can? We slept fitfully, but early in the morning Selene woke me and we made love, abandoned and free.

Later that day I was doing my usual patrol around the store when I saw Betty try on a fur coat that would have cost a fortune. She was watching me through a mirror and I noticed that her eyes were more agitated than usual, but I decided to let her be, hoping that she would leave it back on the stand. Unfortunately, a few minutes later I saw her make her way towards the door, the fur coat still over her shoulders. I quickly moved around the counter to cut her off as she reached the door. "Now, now, Betty," I remember saying as I intercepted her, putting my arm out to prevent her from leaving the store, when suddenly I saw a flash of naked steel as she drove a large kitchen knife into my chest.

God! It had been a shock to say the least. And a damn near miss. Anyhow, I've got over it now and back to work again and trying to get on with life and we're just not thinking too much about the future at all. In fact, we've probably a lot to thank poor old Betty for. Our little Johhny's doing fine and his hair-lip isn't half as bad as mine, and I'm head of Security now, with a pension. In fact, in spite of what that insurance company had said about my bad genes, they did more or less add, that I must have had a lucky gene to be here at all.

Johnny's Decision

Until that letter arrived, we'd been absolutely delighted with John's progress. He had done extremely well in all his assessments and screenings and we were rightly proud of him. His tall slim figure, his straightly held shoulders and blond hair marked him out from the rest of the class and his bright blue eyes sparkled with enthusiasm at whatever he was doing and among his colleagues he seemed always to have a captive audience. Now in senior school he was top of the class and was nearly sure to be elected head boy in his final year. John had great potential and Sarah and I were so proud of him.

Of course, we hadn't taken any risks and unlike some of our neighbours who hadn't bothered to take advantage of the gene screening tests, and we had every expectation that John would be a high flier. We had chosen the *in vitro* fertilisation method of conception that was now of offer by some biotech companies and although expensive Sarah and I felt that since we only wanted to have one child that it would be worth doing our best to ensure that, firstly he would be a boy and secondly that he'd have an A1 genetic profile. Mind you, we missed a holiday that year as a comprehensive *in vitro* fertilisation and selective embryo gene screen was a costly business. However, having an A1 child was a good investment and we got a much better deal on the medical insurance. Admittedly, both Sarah and I had our own problems. Sarah carried the gene for breast cancer, like her mother, and I had a predisposition to take Alzheimer's Disease. However, with the new pre-emptive drug treatment the risks of both conditions developing were reduced to practically zero and it gave us a great deal of confidence. By using *in vitro* fertilisation techniques, we had ensured that John carried none of our bad genes.

Not everyone had been so careful or lucky, and our next-door neighbours had been rather foolish. They hadn't bothered to get a gene screen done before starting a family and had gone ahead regardless of all the medical advice that was now available. The result was only too obvious. One child was mentally retarded, a condition that could easily been diagnosed prenatally and the other was a severe asthmatic and seemed allergic to everything, including our cat should it ever jump over the garden fence. The number of rows we'd had with them about our cat Toby has been enormous and in a fit of rage I once told them frankly, what I thought about them having kids like that when they could have taken some care and been more responsible. I know it was a terrible thing to say, but it was the truth and nobody really appreciates the anguish you can go through when you do want to take care and plan things responsibly.

Of course, since John's birth, the success of the Human Genome Project has been so great that new diagnostic test for novel genes are being marketed every week and John has had an up to date screen done every few years. So far, he's maintained his A1 rating, but it is always an anxious period waiting for the results of the tests and with so many new genes being discovered, you never really know what to expect. In fact, only five others in his class at school have kept their A1 rating and so we feel rightly proud of him, as we all knew that Johnny was the best. Physically, genetically, academically Johnny was at the top of the class and we had no doubt that he would be elected head Boy next year. He was by far the most popular chap with the rest of the boys and always praised by the schoolmasters and we never imagined that there was anything wrong and were more than horrified when the letter arrived.

"Look at this," Sarah said, tossing the letter over the breakfast table to me." We've to get Johnny another gene test."

I read the letter before saying a word, the lump in my throat stopping me from uttering a word. "This is nonsense," I eventually stammered, "this is unbelievable. They can't mean this."

The letter was official. It was from the Regional Sex Orientation Unit that had officers visit every school who examined the sexual development of children. We never had any dealing with this organisation before and it had never entered our heads that Johnny had any problem in the sexual aspects of his life. Sarah and I had a very happy sexual relationship and although Johnny didn't know many girls, as he was at a boys school he'd had a few teenage crushes on girls when on holiday and always seemed a good mixer, although we were sure that as yet he never had had a steady girl friend.

The letter claimed that during their recent survey of the school they had assessed that Johnny had borderline gay tendencies and advised us that a new diagnostic gene test for sex orientation that had just recently become available should be had. It went on to say, "that this information would allow John to decide more logically on his sexual orientation and lead in the long run to a more satisfying and full life experience."

"This is bullshit!" I exclaimed, spilling my cup of coffee over the table as my hand was shaking uncontrollably. "Johnny is no more gay than I am. It's that damn school" I roared on, "Half the staff are gay and they influence the boys every time they get the chance. I always thought we should have sent him to a mixed school. Anyway, he has no gay gene." I said with confidence and realism returning to my voice. "If he has one it must have come from your side," I laughed, trying to ease the tension around the table.

"Just because my brother never married does not mean he was gay," Sarah sparked back.

"I'm sorry, I didn't mean that."

"Yes you did. You always blame me," she retorted sharply.

"It isn't you, I'm blaming. It's the system," I said, as I swallowed my daily tablet that would prevent me from taking Alzheimer's Disease when I was over sixty and reaching over the anti-breast cancer tablet to Sarah who swallowed it with difficulty, tears in her eyes. However, the moment of quiet brought us both back to reality. "Look, if there is a gay gene why is there not a tablet to cure it, like they have for all the other bad genes. Instead of that the system says, No! Don't cure it, it's natural, let's develop it."

"Well maybe they will have a drug soon. You know how fast things move in the pharmaceutical industry." Sarah said quietly, trying to calm me. "Don't worry, Johnny's a sensible boy and we'll talk to him at the weekend. I suppose we had better give permission to have this test done. Anyway, it'll have to be Johnny's decision.

We collected Johnny as usual from the station late on Friday evening. His tall lean figure stepped effortlessly from the carriage, a knapsack packed with books, homework and a weeks worth of dirty clothes hung loosely from one shoulder. He kissed his mother on the cheek and gave me his usual "Hi

Dad" and put his arm around my shoulder, his strong fingers giving me a gentle squeeze.

In the car on the way home he was unusually quiet and seemed to be avoiding talking to us. We sensed it was going to be a difficult weekend. After supper I decided to wait until Saturday, probably during our afternoon walk with the dog, before talking to him about the letter, but Sarah and I both found it difficult to get around to opening up the subject that had plagued us during most of the week and it was Sunday lunchtime before I eventually plunged in while the potatoes were being served.

"We've had a letter from school. They say some people have been talking to you about sex," my eyes firmly fixed on my plate of lamb and carrots and roast potatoes.

"Oh yes, they were around a couple of weeks ago. Didn't say much, just asked us to fill in a questionnaire and gave us a talk on safe sex. We'd heard it all before. They seemed to think we were a bunch of youngsters.

"Was it only a questionnaire?" I asked always dubious about the value of them.

"They talked to a few of us privately after they had looked at our answers. They seemed intrigued that I never have had a steady girl friend. and kept referring to Ian Farlow. You know that he has been my best friend ever since we went to school."

"They suggest that you should have the test for the gay genes that have recently been found. Do you want too?" Sarah asked, knowing that I would never get around to broaching the question.

"Oh yes, they talked a lot about the sex orientation genes that are now known and said that we would soon be able to obtain information as to what life style would be most suitable for us."

"Well, do you want to have the test?" I asked anxiously, sensing that Johnny was many steps ahead of us in his thoughts on this problem.

"Have a gay gene test, Dad! Christ no! Ian and I laughed our heads off after that wee queer gave his talk. Ian said gay gene or no, all we want is to get a good woman. Like the girl, I had on holiday last year. By the way, she says in her letters, that her parents have booked the same chalet for this year, so I hope that we're going there again, too." He leaned over and kissed Sarah on the cheek and when his blue eyes caught mine, they were bright and sparkling with humour and maturity. Johnny had already made his decision and he'd been enjoying his weekend after all.

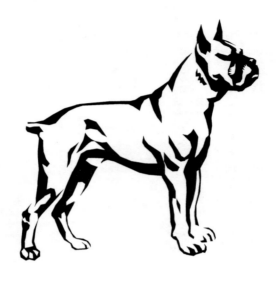

'Hunting Genes'

"June!" I shouted above the babble of the milling crowd that suddenly quietened, sensing the anxiety in my voice. "Have you got Patricia?"

"No, I thought you had her," June called back, as the crowd opened between us like the Red Sea for Moses and we moved unhindered to the centre of the road, anxious faces from across Ireland gathering around to help or others slipping away not to be involved.

Allen gripped my left hand firmly, while our little John held Brockey, tightly by her collar.

"Has anyone seen a small girl with blonded hair, in a red jumper and green shorts?" I asked, my eyes searching over the heads of the milling crowd down the hill.

"What age is she?" a voice asked from the crowd.

"She's nine," June responded quickly, adding hopefully, "Have you seen her?"

There was silence, a mixture of sympathy and ridicule in their eyes. This was no place to lose a wee girl. There were all sorts at the Fair. You'd never know who she'd meet up with. They come from all over and many of them up to no good. A wee lass like that could get trambled in the crowd. There's drunks and hooligans and God knows what types are in the town on a day like this. Sheer carelessness and neglect. They didn't need to say a word. I knew what they were thinking.

"I thought you had her," I said, again, disapprovingly to June, my words wanting someone else to blame. But our moist eyes caught, telling us that we only wanted Tricia back safely. "She'll be all right," I encouraged June, whose face had gone pale behind the summer tan, but my trembling voice told her that I was as worried as she was. A black passing cloud blanked out the late summer sun, bringing a sudden chill to the air. The place was strange, the people, aliens, moving shadows, with sinister, suspicious purpose. The friendly smiles of the locals seemed to have changed to scowls of derision and disinterest. We were alone in a multitude.

We had come down to Ballycastle early that morning from the little mountain farm where we'd parked our caravan for the last few days. Old Jose, the farmer, had talked about the Auld Lammas Fair the previous evening while we sat around the peat fire in his small thatched cottage tucked in a copse of trees on the banks of a river that bore its way down the glen. On leaving in the morning, he had given us friendly advice to watch out for the pickpockets and added casually that a bad lot had started to come to the town from the city these past few years. We had slowly made our way up the hill from the square lingering at the stalls that lined the main street.

In spite of the Troubles, the Auld Lammas Fair at Ballycastle never once stopped people from across Ireland, from Galway or Cork, Limerick and Kildare, from Donegal and Down, Tyrone or Fermanagh or nearby Derry, from joining in the fun of this ancient market. As the day drew on, the main street was thronged with the masses buying and selling, shouting and laughing. The pubs were filled with red-nosed men shouting for more. The alleys and every spare space was packed with sheep and goats, donkeys and horses, chickens and pigeons and every sort of thing that anyone in Ireland could ever want to buy or sell or if not, to give away.

There were gentle folk and hard folk, friendly smiles and scowls. Fun stalls to test the skill of every lad and colleen in the land. There were great mountains of sticky Yellow Man and hay stacks of dulce fresh from the sea. Coconut shies and shooting ranges and Punch and Judy shows and prizes of big dolls and little dolls and cuddly toys. I'd tried my hand and aim at the coconut shy but had failed miserably to win the huge cuddly toy Panda that Patricia had taken a notions for. If only I'd won it perhaps she'd have clung on to it and not strayed away from us.

It seemed that the pubs had been opened since dawn and Guinness and Bushmills had flowed down the throats of young and old, some for the first time. Music filled the air and the voices of the salesmen captured passers by and held them entranced with the flow of their words. Secrets given away for the listening - the next story will be even better - but buy, buy, linger, listen and buy! And indeed the slowly moving, mingling horde of humanity became ladened with bulging plastic bags and the little town became the pulsating core of the spirit of Ireland itself.

Every stall had been filled with things to buy or at least to touch. But look, examine and discard, before the stall owner caught your eye. Because then you were hooked. In front of a hundred onlookers, you were suddenly the centre of attention. Were you going to buy or not? The stall men and women were masters at their trade and seldom did you get away without spending a little if not a lot on something that you didn't want and would never have dreamt of buying anywhere else but at the Auld Lammas Fair.

It was into this whirlpool of life, of buying and selling, drinking and laughing, cursing and swearing, that our little Patricia disappeared.

From the top of the hill, I could see down over the main street and for a moment, I recalled the places we had lingered. I recognized the stall where I had bought the little granite model of the Giant's Causeway to remind us of the exciting visit when we walked along the cliff paths and watched the gulls floating on the upstream of air from the deep gorges where the old Spanish galleons came to grief. How I had held Pat's hand as we edged around the Point on the narrow cliff path, seeing only the deep greeny blue of the sea hundreds of feet below. How could I have let her wander off among the unknown hazards of the Auld Lammas fair?

I continued to scan the crowds in the vain hope of seeing my little Patricia's golden hair catch the sun. Only the multicoloured fluttering flags and the bright balloons, one of which had gone adrift, caught my eye. My mind flashed back to another time when we were on the top of the cliff at Fair Head and above Murlough Bay. There was a good fresh breeze blowing out to sea and we had been flying our red Peter Powel kite with its great long yellow tail curling and twisting and diving, competing with the gulls and great black crows that were angered by the intrusion of the foreign thing into their domain. We got bolder and bolder and dared each other to make fancier turns and more dangerous dives and to 'kiss the waves'. By now, the kite was well out over the sea and then the line snapped. In the first moment of freedom, the bright red kite soared away, taut and beautiful, its long golden tail streaming out behind. Then, its energy spent, it folded and turned and tumbled in chaos into the ocean. Now Patricia was lost in the chaos of a wild Irish carnival.

"We'll go and find her," Allen offered. "She's probably watching the Punch and Judy Show. She's been talking about it all week."

John had been holding Brockey's collar and without saying a word, he slipped the chain over her head.

"Brockey will find her," John suddenly shouted with glee. "Go on, Brockey! Fetch Tricia. Good girl. Go on! Go on! Fetch Tricia."

Of course, it was the natural thing to do. One of Brockey's favourite games was for the children to hide in the forest and then I would release her and she would go running in barking and hunting until she found them among the trees. Brockey's genes were well tuned by generations of breeding to make her a natural hunter. Now in spite of her thorough training and careful nuturing from a pup she was free and away, with her beloved Tricia, her game and quarry.

I tried to catch her. "You're stupid John," I shouted, cuffing his ear. "You shouldn't let her off here." I was embarrassed enough without having to try and catch our big strong boxer in the middle of this crowd. But she was playful and her blood was up. The crowd separated in a ring around us. Brockey barking and jumping and turning and Allen and John and myself all chasing her in circles while the anxious onlookers were cheering and laughing but still half afraid and keeping well out of Brockey's way. However, their fear and excitement was infectious and her blood rose even more.

"Fetch Tricia!" John shouted, ignoring me. "Fetch Tricia!"

Now there was no need for more encouragement. Brockey was away. Free like the kite over the sea, Brockey cut a swathe through the crowd. Hands went out to grab her. But her coat was short and smooth and there was no collar to hold and with a few barks and growls, she was down the Main Street and the Auld Lammas Fair went wild. Stalls pulled to the ground, balloons bursting, piles of unbought cabbages and fruit rolling like footballs down the hill, china crashing and pots and pans clanging and there was shouting and cursing and chasing the whole length of the town.

We followed the chaos down the street, our plastic bags getting bumped and torn and our precious purchases dropping on the road, lost forever. We hastened on, spurred by the cries of derision and abuse from the owners of damaged stalls and others frightened by Brockey's onward uncontrollable flight.

"Control that bloody dog! You idiot." Their words stung my ears and my face was red and sweating and we all were fearing that we would be lynched by the crowd of maddened Irish when suddenly I saw her safe and sound.

She was sitting on the top of a table, outside O'Flattery's Bar, cuddling a huge Panda toy, her golden hair all-blowing in the breeze and her lips all sticky from eating Yellowman.

"Hi, daddy!" Pat called to us as she saw us running up. Brockey was already lying quietly under the table having just finished off a huge bowl of Guinness. "Look who I've found."

One of the big farming men, who was sitting at the table and had come to the Fair for the sheep sale, got up and turned to me.

"Surely to God aye, it's yourself," Jose, our farmer friend from up the mountain, said smiling and grasping my hand and pushing me into a spare seat among his mates around the table. "Here, Missus, come and have a seat," he added to June who arrived holding John and Allen firmly by the hand. "Sure I was just telling me mates here about how ye're camping up at the farm and how wee Patricia helps me bring in the cows every morning. Sure, I won the wee lass the Panda toy at the coconut shy. Surely to God Aye, someone up there must have helped me!"

"It was his wife," one of his mates said from across the table. "She runs the stall."

We all laughed and were grateful for a Guinness or a coke but I looked back up the hill expecting to see some delegation coming to take me and my dog to the gaol. But the havoc had been forgotten and the Auld Lammas Fair was back to the buying and the selling and the music was booming out and it was going to be a merry night.

And Brockey lay snoring, contentedly, but with one eye open, under the table, his wild hunting genes safely locked-up and repressed, but ready to fire and to be in full-flight at a moment's notice.

Ferromites

I was sure that something was wrong when I visited the Pilbara in Western Australia in 2000, but it was only years later that I began to realise that my suspicions had been justified. At first I had been laughed out of court when I mentioned the possibility and my suggestions were taken as a joke and they raised many great roars of laughter in the pub at Marble Bar during that hot stuffy evening when I and the miners tried unsuccessfully to clear the red dust from our throats by consuming near gallons of dark liquid, said to be from faraway Ireland but really made under licence in Melbourne or Perth.

Jack, my assistant and guide, had been a silent type and hardly spoke a word, burying his head in a novel whenever the dust in the cab was clear enough to read. But he knew the land and guided me safely across it, from waterhole to waterhole, from gorge to gorge, down dried up river beds that would be impassable in the Wet. But he was hurt and smouldered with silent anger that the land of his ancestors had been stolen from them and would now be lost forever.

We had spent the dry season up there, surveying the vast semi desert region between the mines and the coast and advising the Company how to develop the scarred mountain of waste rubble that had been dug out from the great iron mines over the last fifty years. But soon iron ore of any commercial value would all be gone and the great man made valleys, some nearly a mile deep would be flooded and used to irrigate the parched plains to the west. A new agricultural paradise was envisaged and the huge plains of western Australia would become fertile and rich, able to support millions of cattle and major crops of grain and fruit. We'd travelled widely across the rugged plains between the mines and Port Headland, surveying and measuring and photographing. At first overcome by the enormity of the gorges of the Hammersley ranges I was soon enjoying the challenge of estimating how best to control the flow of water that from the beginning of time, had rushed during the wet season uninhibited across the high plains and emptied into the Indian ocean, having torn yet more of the red core of Australia apart.

However, although ancient, the land was not dead. After the rains it would become lush and green, sparkling with coloured flowers, that would burst into bloom for a brief short season, until they parched again as the land turned red, with a greyish hue, due to a coarse covering of hardy spinifix. As we drove around in the battered and dusty Discovery, even in the height of the Dry, seeking out the abandoned waterholes, I could see that the land was not dead. Insects and termites were abundant. These scavengers were now steadily eating their way through the dried harvest of the season's brief lushness and building their monuments. Occasionally we would see a coach load of tourists stopping to photograph and to measure themselves against the great edifices, as they stood erect before the strong light of the sinking sun. I had been intrigued with the mounds at first, but as they were so numerous soon I didn't even see them as I drove across the plains.

On the last evening of our trip, we camped by the old railway tract that was used to take the iron ore down from the mines to Port Headland. A waterhole had been marked on the map and around it had developed one of the now abandoned stations that had been used by the workers while the line had been laid. There were a few corrugated iron shacks that had now collapsed and rusty machinery littered the region. Coils of iron cable and tackle were half buried by the red grit and in places covered with the spreading spinifix that had already taken over the flattened area once used as the central square of the simple temporary township. By the side of the track were discarded wagons, tipped on their sides, some with broken wheels or axils, their loads of iron ore, now red with a fine rust, lying where they had been spilt.

We replenished our water containers and ate the last of our supplies, but to morrow night we should be in Marble Bar, which although said to be the hottest place in Australia, would be sure to provide us with the coolest drink on earth as well as soft beds. So, as had become my custom, I spread my ground sheet under the stars and using a convenient pile of fine iron ore gravel as a pillow, nestled into my sleeping bag, dreaming of that cool Guinness the following evening. But I had a restless sleep and once got up and got an insect net which I seldom bothered with, but to night the beasties seem worse that usual. However, it didn't help and I began to fidget even more, turning and tossing until eventually, I was fully awake and sitting up, the full moon filling the place with a ghostly light. I wiped my face that was itchy and saw on my hand hundred of black ants. "God," I gasped. "If these are poisonous, I've had it." I looked down at the sleeping bag and ants were crawling everywhere. Well to be honest, I guess I knew that they were termites, but at that time of night and with the sudden scare of finding them crawling all over me, I just thought of them as ants. Behind me, the wagonload of iron ore that I'd been using as a pillow was covered with them. They were everywhere. All along the railway line, the piles of the enriched iron ore gravel and dust were covered with a frenzy of movement. Just a few metres beyond my feet, on a piece of stony ground, a broad column of blackness, shimmering in the moonlight, flowed past. It disappeared into the spinifix, like oil flowing into grass. I got up, dusting the ants from my clothes and switching on my torch, I followed the plank of termites as they moved across the ground towards the edge of the old encampment. I didn't go far as the ground was alive and I must have crunched thousands of them to death as I walked through the spinifix. In the torchlight, I saw another column surging towards me. It passed underfoot, ignoring my fatal footsteps and shimmered on towards the piles of rust along the rail side. Then I saw it. It was shimmering in the moonlight, metallic, bright in its blackness. The mound was taller than I was and at least twice as broad. Its surface was a molten mass of quivering life. I hit the surface with my torch and it rang like a metal bell.

I ran. Oblivious of the slaughter I was causing I rushed back to my camp site and shaking Jack, who was snoring peacefully, in the back of the Discovery, I jumped in and roared the diesel engine into life, driving out of the encampment leaving a cloud of dust trailing behind me.

We reached Marble bar late the following afternoon, having done little surveying during the final day of our trip. I could write up a reasonable report that would provide the general outline of where a series of dams could be built that would give adequate year round water for an immense regions of the outback. More detailed studies would have to be done but at least my proposal would be a start and if it got approval from the Board, I would have an interesting job for the next few years. However, it was the sight of the termites, not my pending Report that was at the forefront of my mind as I drove that last lap through the desert towards Marble Bar.

"Tell us another one, Sam," was all that I heard from the miners who packed the bar that night as I told of my experiences with the termites the previous evening. "I guess you got too much sun out there at this time of year." Sean Flaggerty, the bar man said more seriously that the others. "They should never have sent a Sydney boy like you out there alone. You're lucky to get back in alive."

"No, No, it's not the heat," I defended my argument. "I'm used to that and I wasn't hallucinating. I tell you those termites are eating iron." I took another long draught of my cool Guinness and wiped my lips, looking briefly to see if any ants were still clinging on to the back of my hand. "I swear to God that they eat iron. More than that they are building bloody iron mounds." Everyone roared making me even more emphatic about my theory that was forming by the second in response to the peer pressure of my drinking colleagues. "The Company has been complaining about running out of iron, for years, but you all know that there is still plenty of iron around. It's just that it's not concentrated enough to make it easy to extract." They were silent and I knew that I'd captured their interest and attention. I went on, speculating as I went, after another draught. "Well I think the Company has got some bright biotechnologist to genetically engineer a iron eating termite and they will go out and bring iron back by the ton from all sorts of places. You boys," I added, without thinking of the impact it would have on the large muscular miners who packed in tightly around the bar listening to the mad blow in from Sydney with his half Irish accent, whose yarns had livened up their lonely existence over the past months, "you boys will be out of a job. Those billions of termites will carry more iron than all your big trucks put together." " Not bloody likely, they won't," laughed a big chap who drove one of the huge trucks that dwarfed even a tourist coach and whose tyres were over twelve feet high. But my jokes struck a chord and the mood of the miners cooled. They knew only to well that soon their jobs were at an end. Soon the mine would close and the whole place flooded and water engineers would replace them. Some would get jobs in the new construction industry that would transform the landscape of the Pilbara and would create a new inland water system that would match what the Chinese had done when they dammed the great gorges of the Yanksee.

Next morning, having shaken hands with Jack and had a mumbled "Good bye," I boarded a small Company plane to Broome and caught the afternoon flight to Perth. Staying at the

Dixon, I felt civilisation return as I looked over the beautiful city, down the Swan River and showered away the dust of the outback, talking and looking at myself in the mirror, remembering Jack's dark and sad eyes that had never once looked on mine. I had to put the final touches to the Report and e-mailed it to the secretary at the Company's head office by seven the next morning. I knew the members of the committee would each have a copy before our meeting the following afternoon.

I arrived shaved, shorn and polished, sure that my report would be greeted with enthusiasm. The committee had already gathered and I was ushered into the room, where the five members, who were silver haired and stern and dressed in dark suits, were studying my report and maps of the region were spread out across the wide polished table.

"Welcome back, Sam. You had a good trip then?" The chairman asked, shaking my hand before I sat down. "How did you get along with Jack? Has he finished that book yet?"

"Indeed, he's a quiet chap. Hasn't much to say but he knows the desert all right. Couldn't have done without him."

"Well now," he continued, his colleagues looking at me over their spectacles, their faces stern, and lips drawn. "Your report looks good and congratulations. This will be very useful, but before talking about it I have to ask about something else."

"What is it?" suddenly aware that something was not quite right. There was an atmosphere in the room that made be feel cool.

"Apparently you made a claim in Marble Bar that the Company was using genetically engineered termites. Is that true?"

I swallowed and my throat felt dry. Thousands of termites seemed to be stalking across the table towards me. "Well I did get spooked one night out in the desert and I joked about it in the bar, but surely nobody took me seriously."

"Well Sam, unfortunately you've caused a strike up at the mine and the whole place is at a standstill the morning."

"Christ," I said, "That's awful, I didn't mean that to happen. I was only making a joke. I suppose I'd drunk to much, but you know what it's like after being in the desert for weeks." I tried to find excuses but realised that the members were not impressed. The Company would be losing thousands every hour that the production stopped and if the anti GM brigade got control of the miners, there'd be hell to pay. I was doomed, termites or no termites.

"Of course we know you were joking but you gave them just the excuse they wanted and God know what the Greenies will do now they'll got hold of it. We want you to sign this declaration saying that it was just your imagination being in overdrive. This might help to stop the miners panicking any further. Anyway. It's a mess and there is no way we can take you on to continue with the project. We'll pay you for the report and advice, but we want you to go back to Sydney and stay out of Western Australia until the dust settles. Here's a first class ticket to Sydney on the next flight out this afternoon. Don't talk to any reporters or you'll be made to look the biggest joke in Australia." I felt like a schoolboy being reprimanded for playing a plank and was about to respond, when the chairman, standing up and handing me over the tickets, added coolly, "and by the way, you won't get the commission for the report until this damn strike is over."

I was escorted by two hefty men out of the back of the building and by car sped to the airport and by passing the check-in desks was led directly to plane, the body guards sitting beside me, avoiding all possible contacts with any reporters who may have been looking for me. I was assured that my baggage, that I had left in the Dixon Hotel would be sent on to me and I joked that I hoped they'd keep any termites they found as there may well have been some trapped in my sleeping bag. My escorts hadn't even smiled and like Jack sat silent until they left shortly before take-off.

Back in Sydney I had a few sleepless nights, but within the week my declaration seem to have worked and the strike ended with promises of even better compensation for any miners who could not be employed by the new water development company that was in the process of buying the old mine. I got my commission and continued with my lecturing job, forgetting about my ambition about making a fortune in industry. But naturally I kept my eye on the developments in the Pilbara and saw many of my suggestions become a reality over the years as the new water development scheme slowly transformed the landscape and opened up the region to agriculture and industry, encouraging a surge of immigration from the bulging populations in the islands to the north.

I have retired now and living on the north of the harbour, with a glorious view over the bay to the Opera House and the ever spectacular Harbour Bridge. A headline report in the Sunday morning paper about a major catastrophe in Perth attracted my attention as I perused the thick wad of paper that had just been delivered. The Dixon Hotel had collapsed. Hundred of people had been killed and the place was in chaos.

Some said it was terrorists, others a gas explosion, but suddenly I knew it was the termites.

The reporter had mentioned similar unexplained collapses occurring all along the west coastal towns and cities during the past twenty years. He had catalogued them and with their dates showed clearly that the occurrences were becoming more frequent and were spreading southwards and northwards from the Pilbara. Of course, I realised that in the Pilbara, all the townships and mining buildings themselves had long since been flooded and submerged under the new lakes and dams, but where had the termites gone? Had I taken a few by accident to the Duxton during my brief stay all those years ago and they escaped from by baggage and set up a colony in the foundations of the hotel, breeding growing and eating their way up the metal infrastructure. Had some of my unwanted passengers been returned to Sydney along with my baggage and set up colonies here? In those days, I lived in a flat at the Rocks, just under the harbour bridge. I remember throwing my sleeping bag in a pile in the corner of the basement, never wanting to use it again. It is probably still lying there, probably now a pile of dust, eaten by vermin maggots or termites.

Over the years, I had heard a lot about what the genetic engineers had done with micro-organisms to make them useful for industry, just as medics had developed them for use in the new medicines, which we all were only too glad to have as protection against the ever-increasing hordes of antibiotic resistant bacteria and virus diseases. I'd read that even stranger bugs have been found, deep under the ground and in the oceans. Bugs that have eaten the *Titanic* wreck and turned it within a century into a mound of inorganic sludge. Bugs that use iron ore instead of oxygen to burn the carbon used for food. Bugs that can eat concrete and caused the collapse of the Cairo sewers soon after they were built. With the genetic technology, genes from these rare organisms were switched and swapped until new strain was made to suit the wishes of industrialists. Some of these, often called GEMS, were used to help clean up the environment and remove pollution, others to make the extraction of rare minerals more economic. I realised as I read the newspapers reports on the collapse of the Dixon, that the Company in the Pilbara had probably not, as they had said, experimented with termites, as I had foolishly suggested, but they may well have been involved with some of the novel GEMS. What if the termites had come to use these GEMS for their own benefit? Their tiny guts carrying a flora of gems that gave them the necessary enzymes to digest iron.

I lifted the phone to contact one of my academic colleagues who would know about these things, but it was too late. I looked over the veranda railings prompted by a fierce noise and screeching coming up from the Bay. The Harbour Bridge was tilting and twisting, the great curved loops of metal springing into the air and the whole bridge collapsing towards the Rocks. That's my end I thought. What have I done?

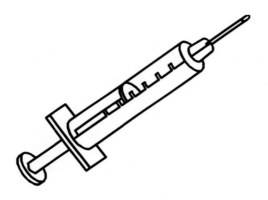

SUPERBUG

Fiona realised that she'd been conscious for sometime, her mind gradually surfacing from a dream, her senses beginning to function, slowly recognising clinical smells and flowered curtains and the hum of an electric fan that blew cool air on her hot face. She'd no pain and she wondered if it had happened or if she just been asleep and was still waiting to be taken to theatre. Above her head, she saw the telling dark red plastic bag. At the side of her bed was a machine that was blinking and bleeping. "It's over," she said to herself. "Thank God, it's over."

A nurse came through the folds of the curtain and smiled, taking Fiona's hand in hers. "You're awake, then?" she said smiling. "How do you feel?"

"Ok. I've no pain."

"You've had a epidural. You won't feel anything for a few hours. If it gets sore later, I give you something for it. We can take this off you now," the nurse said as she removed the connections to the monitor. "You're back to nornal already. You'll be on your feet in no time," she laughed. "Your Mum and Dad have just arrived. Can you see them now? I'll bring you a cup of tea. It will help to revive you."

Fiona raised herself slightly in the bed and braced herself for the pending visit. They'd be shocked, worried stiff, mortified, and angry! They would have come across from Belfast to Heathrow and then by coach to Cambridge. It was a long trip. Mother would be exhausted. Father would be fuming.

Mother came in first, the nurse pulling back the curtains and arranging chairs on either side of the bed. "Are you all right, darling," leaning over and kissing Fiona on the forehead, holding her hand in a tight loving grip.

"You've been in the wars, then," her father said, kissing her cheek and sitting down heavily on the small plastic chair.

"I'm sorry Dad, I didn't mean this to happen."

"We know, dear. You'll be all right. That's the main thing."

Her Father had already seen the surgeon and knew all about the operation and had been told what had happened so they didn't stress Fiona with questions about the accident. It could have been worse. But why did she have to go and join that lot? Surely to God, there was plenty to do at College without getting involved with cranks who run around the country tearing up cabbages and ruining people's crops. Fiona's father was a farmer in County Antrim, and hated the idea of a crowd of well meaning do gooders crashing they way across his precious fields of barley or wheat, claiming they were saving the world.

Fiona was in her second year at Cambridge and her father and mother had been delighted at her success. She seemed enjoying her student life. But she'd never mentioned being involved in any campaign or being political. "How did you become involved with these people?" he eventually asked when he was sure that Fiona was willing to talk.

"Well, you know that I've always been interested in the environment and making sure that you didn't pour pig slurry into the river and so on. Not like grandfather used to do. Well, now they're growing GM crops all over the place and we don't know what long-term effects these new plants will have. They say they are controlled experiments but they're not. They are out in the open country and there is nothing to stop them spreading."

"But surely, the farmers and the scientists know what they're doing. There might be a risk, but it must be very small. There's a risk in everything we do. We can't have a risk-free world, my dear."

"It's not just the risk." Fiona answered sharply, beads of sweat breaking on her forehead. "It's wrong!" She pulled the sheet up tightly under her chin and frowned, feeling a twinge of pain at her ankle. "They shouldn't be swapping genes around and making all sorts of organisms that were never meant to be. It's all immoral. They're trying to play God. They'll be making designer babies next."

"Well I wouldn't want to go as far as that," her mother agreed, "there's been so many changes in our day that I wonder when it will ever stop."

The nurse who had been hovering around came over and took Fiona's hand and after a monment, said quietly that they should let her rest now. They both kissed their daughter and said they'd be back later. They'd reserved a room in a small hotel but still had to go and get booked in.

Fiona was glad they'd gone. She had known that her father would not have approved of her becoming a member of the anti-GM League. She'd never dreamt that she would have become physically involved, but despite attending numerous demonstrations and parades, nothing seemed to stop the introduction of more and more so-called novel crops and farm animals. In response, the leading activitists became more and more polarised and they gained support from other environmental and religious groups, especially with the creationists. The more successful biotechnologists became the more extreme the GM Leaguers grew and the argument shifted from considerations of safety and risk onto firm moral grounds.

****

As she tried to doze, resisting the ache that was gradually creeping up her leg, her mind flashed back to the previous morning. There had been a frenzy of excitement as she and her friends form the College Club boarded the coach and headed for the Linconshire plains. They laughed and joked as they struggled into their white biohazard suits and mock facemasks. Some had brought along plastic imitation breathing canisters that would be strapped to their backs and hopefully seem on TV so as to indicate the dangers that they were all taking in the name of the common, innocent, exploited people of Britain. There were cheers and mounting excitement as coach loads of white clad ecowarriers disembarked along an isolated lane beside a field of recently planted cauliflowers that was surrounded by a high wire fence. It didn't matter to them that this was the first large scale trial of a new genetically engineered cauliflower that carried selected genes of the malaria parasite and would probably provide the best vaccine that had ever been made against malaria. If this experiment worked and pending clinical trials were as successful as the WHO scientists anticipated, then the new vaccine would save the lives of millions of people worldwide.

"That won't keep much in or out," one of the young men said, as he cut a way through the fence with sharp cutters. Along with her friends, Fiona had rushed into the field, tearing up the young healthy plants with a sharp pitch fork, turning them in, scattering them, stamping on them, killing them as best she could. The white clad figures were widely spread across the field when Fiona had heard the siren of the police cars racing up the main road a few hundred yards away. Running to catch up with her friends Fiona tripped and fell, rolling over on her back, still holding the heavy fork. One of the police cars, a big fourwheel drive, had crashed through the wire fence and was racing over the field towards her. She staggered to her feet as the wagon bounced across the rough ground, practically now on top of her. Terrified and beyond herself, she threw the pitchfork at the oncoming wagon and as she turned to run she tripped again over a boulder. The young driver, excited and thrilled on his first mission after the ecoterrorists, spontaneously swung away from the oncoming missile but the sharp points of the fork hit the wind screen, shattering it beyond repair as his off side wheel struck Fiona where she'd fallen and ran over her foot. Her screams brought everyone and everything in the field to an abrupt halt.

****

The nurse gave her an injection to ease the pain and said the leg would be sore for a few days but the operation had gone well and she would be OK. The young policeman, who had accidentally run over her and was now sporting a badly bruised eye, had called into to see her in next morning. It was nice of him. Her father wanted to sue him but Fiona didn't want to think about that. It had been a stupid accident. They were both at fault.

But the pain hadn't eased and the following day she had a temperature. The surgeon had spent a long time examining the wound and they took sample after sample and blood tests galore.

"Is anything the matter?" her mother would ask of any passing medic or nurse, but their answer was always, "No. No. Everything's under control."

But Fiona knew it wasn't. By the next morning, her stump felt like a red-hot poker. "You've got a little bit of infection, dear," the nurse said quietly, as though she didn't want anyone else to hear, "We'll give you some antibiotic that will clear it up within a few days."

But the antibiotic didn't work. Fiona had a sleepless night and sweated and ached, her whole body shaking with a fever that added to the pain of her leg, made it near intolerable. The surgeon was with her early in the morning. The tests had come back from the laboratory. It was bad news. She had contacted a hospital super bug that was resistant to all the usual antibiotics. She would have to be moved to an isolation ward and she could only see visitors through a protective plastic screen. However, they said that as she was young and healthy, her own immune system would fight it. They would give her a few days to see if she could beat the bug herself. Her father and mother sat patiently, watching through the plastic protective wall. Poor Fiona was getting worse. Her face was flushed and she sweated, her temperature soaring.

"Is there nothing you can do?" Father asked the surgeon on the third day. "Surely there is some drug you have that could help."

"It's very difficult," the surgeon explained, in a quiet voice, sitting beside them in a nearby alcove, drinking a cup of coffee. "You see, these so-called super bugs have evolved very rapidly, mainly due to the over use and abuse of antibiotics. They mutate and reproduce very rapidly and they are very widely spread, especially in hospitals and in the soil. The truth is that we now have a major crisis and we have no antibiotics of the older type that work any longer."

"What do you mean? What is this older type about? Is there a newer type?"

"Well yes there is, but it is not fully tested yet and hasn't got full clinical approval. We're only allowed to use it if it is a very serious situation and if we have the patients approval."

"Use it! For God sake, use it. I'll give you any approval you need. She's my daughter. If you think it might give her a chance, use it."

"Well now, I'm sorry, but it is not as easy as that. I only wish it was. But this new a drug is produced by genetically engineered methods. The drug is produced by a gene that is actually derived from ants. As you know, ants live in large colonies and yet are very resistant to bacterial infections because they have a natural defence chemical that protects them. Imagine an infection getting into an ant hill," he laughed, trying to ease the tension and let the reality of the situation sink in. "They transferred this ant gene into a yeast so that it can be grown in large quantity. Just like brewing."

"I don't care whether it's genetically engineered from old Nick himself," the father said, "and certainly not from a wee ant. Use it man and be done with it,"

"God, I only wish I could," the surgeon said, reaching into the folder on his lap and removing a sheet of paper. "You see, it is not your decision. It's Fiona's. She's an adult and when she came into hospital, she was asked to sign this form. In fact, she insisted in signing it. It's the new standard consent form for all operations and treatment under the NHS. Here's a copy. She insisted on signing the declaration that she did not want to be fed with or treated with any substance that was derived by means of genetic engineering." He handed the form to the father who read it intensely, his hand shaking as he passed it over to his wife.

"But surely this doesn't apply now. I'm here. I'm her father, I can over rule that."

"I'm afraid you can't," the surgeon said quietly. "You can see that she choose to sign the optional second paragraph. It was her clear and conscious decision. I've explained the situation to her every day this week. She does not want to change her mind. The only way is for me to get a court order to be able to break that request, but the Law will probably treat this as it would someone on hunger strike. Anyway, we are rapidly running out of time. I will ask for that if you wish but first you must try and get her to change her mind. I'm afraid there is nothing I can do if your daughter doesn't want to change her mind. I'm very sorry, but it is up to you." He rose, his voice lowering a tone and and looking down at them he added, "you know that the crop they destroyed wasn't GM food, it was a Biomedic Crop and would have provide a million doses of malaria vaccine. Probably would have saved the lives of thousands of children." He patted them both on the shoulders left them gazing at the copy of Fiona's declaration.

They moved back to the bedside and looked at their daughter through the plastic protective screen. She seemed to be asleep and looked more peaceful. The flush had gone from her face. Her father's mind was in a whirl. That could explain her talking about children dying when Fiona had been delirious the previous evening. But, maybe she had beaten the super bug after all and would recover. Maybe she was right. Maybe we do depend too much on drugs instead of our immune system that was made to protect us against infections. They held her hands through the plastic. They were cool. They waited for her to wake.

Adventures in Viroland*

Once upon a time little Bev** was cast up on the shore of Viroland. That evening a storm had blown his ship, *The Cow,* away off course and after a particularly violent gust of wind, she had been completely shattered with all hands lost, except for sturdy little Bev. Bev only managed to survive the rough passage ashore because he was such an extremely hardy little chap. He could survive in salty water or fresh. He could be dried out and frozen and some even thought he could be boiled, but no matter what life asked him to put up with, he always managed to be around.

In Viroland, he soon became very popular due to his easygoing sense of humour and his ability to get along well with really anyone. In fact even the most inexperienced and silly people never really did him any harm. Bev just loved to fool around. He spend a lot of time rolling in circles and playing table tennis and even tried his hand at model building, but he was best at getting new techniques going. He was always up to date with the latest fashion in genes and he never turned an eye at becoming completely integrated with computers and the like. Within a few years, little Bev had established himself as key figure in Viroland and felt very happy and secure. Life had never been so good. Gone were the days when he had been a slave to *The Old Cow*. He was glad he'd seem her go to the bottom in pieces that awful night long ago.

But then Mae Sells*** arrived. Unlike Bev who had come unseen and had quietly and usefully got himself involved practically unnoticed by his new colleagues, Mae Sells arrived with a flourish. Everyone knew she was coming, and the excitement mounted. She was already well established in the international scene, and she knew it. Even the world Press announced it, intrigued that Viroland was taking on such a Lady. Of course, Mae Sells's name was notorious. She had been around for a long time and had been in the vanguard of conquests of the New World and had devastated the native populations well before the European armies added their final unslought. Now she was on the rampage again. The world looked on in fear. She had become persistent. Nevertheless, in spite of her history, Mae Sells was welcomed with open arms. She was very rich. Her cloak sparkled with diamonds and gold leaf and everyone wanted to see her on stage. Her photograph was passed round and the new word *collaboration* was introduced.

Little Bevy had anticipitated her arrival as much as anyone. He was intrigued with her reputation and was sure that they'd become good friends. After all, he had with everyone else, so why not with Mae Sells. He would show her a few tricks and keep her amused and with luck, with her money and his brains they would conquer the world! However, Mae Sells had other plans. From the start little Bev was ignored, that is except when he was useful, which was quite often, especially at the beginning, but in reality, Bev was pushed to the sidelines. Mae Sells had become a star. She attracted international attention, and visitors from as far away as Japan came to see her and European collaboration became firmly established. Her close cousin Canny Distemper joined the group and together they would conquer the world!

But little Bev had a very positive attitude. He survived and in spite of everything, he prospered. His native stability proved a great bonus to structural studies and he got exposure to the most powerful circles in the world. He got fried to nothing but still he was on the Internet. He was also easily manipulated and he was cut up and sown up and swapped around until the poor little fellow hardly knew where he was or who he was. However, it was all in a good cause. He was to make something of himself. After all little Bev had never been a trouble. He was an innocent by-stander in the world of others like Mae Sells. Now with all this manipulation he could become useful. At last, he could carry useful bits of other things, even bits of Mae Sells and become the biotechnologists dream.

But Mae Sells had other plans. She had tired of her strong negative image and wanted to improve it and become more positive. Her glittering coat shimmered with excitement when she thought of her change to a positive pathway in life. Could she become respectable, make up for all the evil she'd caused, even be able to carry useful bits of other things and become the biotechnologists dream............

.... and I woke up with a violent tug, the setting sun shining in my eyes and a large fish jumping at the end of my line.

*A dream of a retired virologist.

**Bev is short for Bovine Enterovirus

***Mae Sells is a Belfast pronouncation of Measles.

A NEW PAIR OF GENES *

As you can imagine my wife and I were delighted and highly honoured to learn of the award of a personal chair in gene biochemistry. Unfortunately our euphoria was short-lived as our boys were soon to draw our attention to the following heading in the local evening newspaper

"Now Gene Jokes go on Record"

I have been warned by a previous speaker from this platform that audiences at inaugural lectures are much too clever to be hoodwinked -but "I am glad to see that you are not too clever to be amused".

Alternatively, I may of course have had to say, "I am *sad* to see that you are also too clever to be amused". Here we see in these simple statements, that meanings can be drastically altered by minor changes in words or the order of letters - this is the essence of Gene Biochemistry.

The theme I would like to pursue this evening is that *life* is a language based on the order or sequence of bases or building units which make up the molecules of nucleic acids or as they are now commonly known, DNA or RNA. I will try and show how we have learned the alphabet of this genetic language, how we have learned to read and write in the language and how recently, with the advent of recombinant DNA or genetic engineering procedures we are beginning to write creatively -though at present rather like a child struggling with his first essay or perhaps a new professor composing his inaugural lecture - and so towards my title, "A New Pair of Genes".

I would, if I may, compare the development of this gene science with a river flowing down an Irish glen. Often the waters flow fast, bubbling brown with excitement, over rapid and fall, plunging into dark unfathomable pools of deep mysteries. Science flows on, unaware seemingly of the scientists, who, too often, are carried along as mere logs, buffeted, worn and sometimes left stranded on dry banks unnoticed and forgotten. But the river grows, the confluence of tributaries, the acquisition of new material, until eventually, in full spate, it plunges forth into the oceans, the waters ladened with acquired knowledge, much of it silt, that sinks and gathers moss on continental shelves - but much also providing nutrient and food for thought in the world at large - our science becomes a technology.

This river that I have had the privilege of fishing in for the past 40 years has a fascinating landscape to paint and I can do no other than start in that tremendous pool high in the hills of science, with the discovery of the laws of inheritance by Gregor Mendel in 1866.

A brief history of the gene

Mendel, whose work as you may recall lay on those dry banks and went unnoticed for some 50 years, had shown by careful quantitative experiments on pea plants that specific characteristics, such as shape, texture, colour, were controlled by two unit factors, one derived from each parent. It was not Mendel, but Wilhelm Johannsen in 1909 who first used the word GENE to describe these hypothetical inheritable factors.

However, the starting point for understanding genes was the realization by Sutton that genes were probably on chromosomes, the thread-like organelles that had been found to be present in the nuclei of all cells. In his paper entitled "The Chromosomal Theory of Heredity" Sutton drew together two completely separate scientific disciplines, the study of inheritance by breeding of plants and animals, and the laboratory based study of single cells by the use of microscopes. It was this hybrid science, a fusion between classical genetics and cytology that laid the bases for modern molecular genetics.

During the next 30 years the science of chromosome analysis was developed, especially by Morgan and his colleagues in America in a study of the fruit-fly, *Drosophila.* This small insect has four large chromosomes in its salivary gland cells and it was possible to relate morphological changes such as eye colour, size of wing, to particular bands that could be stained on these chromosomes. Their work confirmed the concept that genes were physical units arranged in a linear manner along these thread-like structures. All this was consistent with Mendel's concept, as the chromosomes also existed in pairs, one derived from each parent.

Such was the state of our knowledge of genetics around 1940. At that time, when physicists were beginning to fathom the mysteries of the atom and just about to create novel elements by the processes of nuclear fission and fusion, biologists were merely scratching the surface of the huge dictionary of Life - of the secret language of genetics, that in 1940 was unopened and unread. To day, only 40 years later, this dictionary has been prised open for everyone to read and the implications are indeed far-reaching.

During the early 1940's new initiatives were taken and important new approaches made to study the molecular organization of genetic material. Much of the stimulus for this was not from the classical biologists of the day but from men of atomic physics, who for various reasons turned their attention away from the quantum theory and the atom to the gene.

In particular I mention the late Max Delbruck who has been called the father of molecular biology. On arriving in America from Europe in the late 30's, the physicist Delbruck started to work on single-cell organisms, the bacteria and their viruses. He was soon to establish a school of thought and an approach to the study of living things that has led directly to the development of molecular biology as a major force in science today. This was the turning point, the decision of geneticists to turn from the farmyard and the greenhouse to the test tube and the petri dish - to ask simple questions of simple organisms, where the answers could be understood in common physico-chemical terms.

It was the study of bacterial systems that first demonstrated that the chemical known as DNA was the genetic material. This major discovery was made by Avery, McCleod & McCarty in 1944. They studied two strains of bacteria, one of which was virulent and can kill mice and the other non-virulent. They extracted and purified the DNA of the virulent strain and inserted this into the harmless bacterium and were able to obtain transformation of one type of bacterium into the other.

They showed that the DNA alone was able to transfer the characteristic of virulence into the harmless strain. Their experiments drew attention to NUCLEIC ACIDS which up until then had been sadly neglected by chemists and biochemists.

In 1952, Hershey and Chase showed by a series of beautiful experiments that the genes of bacterial viruses or, as they are called, bacteriophages, were also made of DNA and set the scene for much of the work on the fundamentals of how genes replicate and function. This bacteriophage has been studied extensively for many years and its structure has many interesting features, which illustrate how viruses behave in general. The head is made of a protein shell and inside there is a long strand of DNA containing about 50 genes. The fibers provide a means of attachment of the virus to the cell surface and the tail acts as a syringe-like mechanism that can inject the DNA through the cell wall. Only the DNA enters the cell and the protein structures are left on the outside. Once inside the cell the virus genes produce a biochemical "coup d'etat" and redirects and reprogrammes the cell to make only viral proteins and nucleic acids. During a very short period of time, only a few minutes, virus-specific proteins are formed and many thousands of new viral DNA molecules are replicated. The proteins come together to form new particles, surrounding the DNA molecules. The progeny virus particles are released from the dying cell and these experiments showed clearly that virus DNA was able to replicate inside living cells and that the DNA alone was necessary to provide the genetic information for the synthesis of new virus proteins.

I believe that we see here many similarities between the behaviour of these simple genetic systems, the viruses, and the behaviour of man in how he often exploits the biosphere and may even one day exploit outer space. Perhaps in this microcosm of the cell one can learn something of our own nature. I have often referred to viruses as being invaders of the genosphere as only while inside living cells do they take on the essential characteristics of living things. When a genosphere is no longer able to support virus life, they must leave to seek fresh planets to invade, their genes safely encapsulated and protected, frozen into shape, held rigid and inert, as they speed across the intercellular space - hoping to find a new home.

So from the early 1950's with the discovery that DNA was the chemical responsible for heredity, the pace of our river quickens and perhaps as a young schoolboy and student my log was caught up in the current and has been swept along ever since.

The genetic language

The alphabet of this genetic language became resolved by Watson & Crick in 1953 when they established the structure of DNA. The importance is not so much the famous double helix, but rather the concept that two strands are involved in which the sequence of the building units or bases in one strand is related to that in the other. The strands are complementary. The chemical structures need not concern us, merely their symbols or letters A, C, G, T. It was the realization that these bases could form pairs - now known as base-pairs - A in one strand always pairing with T in the other and C with G - that gave the chemical clue to the whole of modern molecular genetics. This tremendous ability and specificity for base-pairing between these four fairly simple chemicals provided the physico-chemical explanations of both how genes replicate and how they function.

The idea that a single gene would have a unique sequence of bases, containing perhaps 500-1000 base-pairs was soon to take root. In that the difference between genes was entirely dependent on the sequence of letters, our analogy with language began to develop. We can reasonably consider a gene as a sentence perhaps 500 letters long; mutations, or changes in genes, can be understood by a change of a letter, a deletion, an addition or a substitution.

Gene replication

Just as in literature a good sentence, a good poem, a useful textbook, or an exciting novel will survive by reprinting, so successful genes can replicate. They do this in a beautifully simple manner. By use of the complementary relationship of the sequence of bases in one strand to the other, the double helix can open up and the parental strands used as templates to allow the monomeric building blocks to be arranged into new daughter molecules of identical sequences.

In their two short communications in 1953, Watson and Crick had elucidated the structure of the genetic material and shown how the information could be passed down from generation to generation. Who could resist angling in a pool bubbling with such excitement?

Gene function: protein biosynthesis

During the 1960's our river turned its attention to how genes function and how proteins are synthesised. Proteins are long chains of amino acids and the problem of protein synthesis is that at least 20 different amino acids must be linked together in a particular order which is determined by the sequences of bases in the gene or DNA.

We now understand gene function in terms of two important words -transcription and translation. Reverse transcription is a rare occurrence which is confined to a single group of viruses. In the normal process, one strand of DNA, the coding strand, is copied into messenger RNA. In messenger RNA each group of three bases is called a codon which codes for a specific amino acid by a process called translation.

Translation is a complex process and occurs in particles called ribosomes which are present in all cells. Ribosomes act as a kind of assembly machine that ensures that amino acids are aligned in a specific order and linked together in a sequence wholly determined by the sequence of letters in the messenger RNA, and hence the gene.

In many ways, protein synthesis is a type of gene amplification, a good example of which is the formation of a strand of hair. In the formation of each hair many millions of protein molecules are produced by a single gene specifying hair protein. In order to do so, this gene makes many thousands of messenger RNA molecules, each of which many thousands or perhaps millions of hair proteins during the life of the hair producing cell.

This ability of genes to function by producing large amounts of proteins and enzymes that could alter and affect the environment was the vital step in starting the process of clothing the naked planet earth with the biosphere we know today. Our analogy with language does not end with the gene being compared to a sentence. We can consider groups of genes functioning as paragraphs and chapters, of whole books, copied and spread around the world, influencing the environment and our culture. I have always been intrigued by C. P. Snow's famous dilemma of the *TWO CULTURES*. I suggest that nowhere do the ARTS and SCIENCES fuse more closely than in the practice and understanding of gene biochemistry. Information and ideas: transfer and storage: retrieval and propagation are indeed the essence of Life, whether it is genetical, at the level of molecules and the cell, among individuals, between nations, or across generations.

Of course, the success of language lies in the fact that it provides the means to cross-fertilise, swap ideas, modify and simplify, extend and recombine concepts and philosophies. In genetics we see that nucleic acid molecules (DNA and RNA) had devised ways of doing this long before man appeared on earth.

Gene transfer in simple organisms.

One of the simplest and best understood genetic systems is a small virus called Lambda. This can have two effects on the bacterial cells it infects. Like other viruses it invades the cell and replicates, producing many hundreds of new particles, killing the cell in the process. Alternatively, the virus genes become integrated with the chromosome of the bacterium and under these conditions the cells do not die and new particles are not produced. Although this arrangement can be quite stable, sometimes the Lambda genes can be cut out or excised from the host chromosome and then the virus can replicate. However, during this excision, the lambda can steal a neighbouring gene belonging to the host cell. This cellular gene is also incorporated into infectious particles and can be transferred to other cells. In fact, the phage can pick up a new pair of genes - these are naturally occurring recombinant DNA molecules.

Similar tranfers can happen in most bacterial cells by small circular chromosomes called Plasmids. These are small circular molecules of DNA about 5000 base-pairs long. Unlike viruses they do not have a protein coat and rather than killing or harming the bacterial cell they often provide very useful genes, such as those that provide resistance to antibiotics or have the ability to utilize unusual chemicals for food. Imagine the benefits to primitive cells, struggling for survival, if genes could be stolen and swapped and amplified and transferred and recombined to form novel useful combinations that may have completely different functions. Indeed viruses may have played a vitally important role in exploring the various genetic possibilities, by encouraging recombination exchange and rearrangements of genes in prehistoric times. Again, just as in literature we see the repeated usage of certain constructions, ideas and phrases, reorganized and remodelled over and over again, to create completely different situations, so in genetics, once the language had reached a certain degree of complexity, an explosion of novelty began to occur by selective recombination and successful exchange. This is a feature of molecular evolution of perhaps far greater importance than the slow accumulation of point mutations, so often a stumbling block in the appreciation of evolutionary theory.

Genetic manipulation techniques

It is perhaps not surprising that within this framework of molecular genetics, with the knowledge of how genes could be manipulated by certain microorganisms, that artificial methods of constructing recombinant DNA molecules were developed. Recombinant DNA or Genetic Manipulation procedures were developed around 1974 following the discovery of enzymes called RESTRICTION NUCLEASES. These enzymes were able to cut DNA at particular sequences. Some cut the double strand in a staggered manner so that STICKY ENDS were produced. By mixing bits of DNA with sticky ends from different sources they can be made to link together and can then be joined in a permanent manner by a joining enzyme called a ligase to form artificial recombinant DNA molecules. These 'artificial' recombinant DNA molecules or genes can then, by use of very standard procedures of growing and cloning bacterial cells, be multiplied and obtained in quantities never before possible, leading to day to the ability of the complete determination of the sequence of the human genome and many other species, and also to the purification of specific genes and their transfer to other organisms including animal and plants. This has led to a revolution in our understanding of biology and medicine and to the rapidly growing biotechnology industry.

Biotechnology

As mentioned in Chapter One, it is only twenty-five years since the start of genetic engineering. How far have we come since the dawn of the new Gene Age? How far will we go until the potential of the gene revolution is fully realised? Twenty years ago it was said that society was at a cross roads, that the new knowledge of molecular biology heralded a new dimension to our lives, unfortunately, like many developments in science the hype of the media and the expectations of the general public often far outruns the reality of the science itself and the hopes and aspirations of the scientists most involved in the developments. As a boy, I was enthralled by the belief that atomic energy would provide the solution to all the earth's energy problems. Then came the scare of radiation and of radioactive waste and the gradual awareness that to eek out the power of the atom for everyday use was a process, far exceeding the original expectations. To destroy a city by the power of the atom was feasible, but to heat a city by the power of the atom was excessively expensive. Then in the mid 1970's, the gene revolution was suddenly upon us. It was predicted that new genetically engineered organisms would turn water into wine, produce ethanol from grass and turn desserts into fertile plains that could feed the world, gene therapy would cure the most difficult of genetic ailments and new drugs and vaccines would eliminate infectious diseases. Is it fair or reasonable to ask the question, what has gone wrong? What has happened or not happened that has prevented all these great and noble expectation from being realised within the working lifetime of the small group of biologists who initially made the gene cloning breakthrough in the early 70's? This is not a question that is very popular among many biologists and especially geneticists, but is often heard on the lips of other scientists, politicians and industrialists who are motivated by the concepts of wealth creation and who have little understanding of the complexities or the timescale of biological engineering. In reality, progress has been very rapid and research students to day are using technologies and devising experiments that would have been undreamt off even five years ago. In fact, progress has been so rapid that two worlds have emerged. The real world, of what is going on in laboratories and institutes and talked among scientists at conferences and published in scientific journals; and the world of perceptions, the world, where the general public hears about new discoveries or developments, which very often are hardly out of the test tube, let alone weaned or even at the toddling stage, and whose long term potentials are explored in detail without any real knowledge or thought about the timescale or experimental complexities involved in the extrapolation of original research into practice.

Let us look back briefly at the history of science and technology and consider the change that has occurred in recent years due to the more open and transparent communication, involving the Press and more importantly, the television. Imagine the situation just over a hundred years ago, when Edison installed the first electric power plant in the world. Let us assume that his invention would have been treated in the same degree of critical analysis, as the discovery of a schizophrenia gene would be today. The hype would be immense. Light and heat in every home; cheap and clean transport and travel; communication and industrial development by machines that would save men's labour. But, on the down side there would be the dangers of transferring kilowatts of electricity around the country; animal and humans being killed by electric shock. Suicide would become too easy. The electric chair would be used instead of the rope. Electric shocks would be used in place of fences and canes. School children kept in order by the teacher pressing a button on the desk consol that would shock an errand child back to order. In this doomsday scenario where can we stop? The ability of our human minds to speculate on the calamitous aspects of any invention far exceeds our ability of creating utopias. It is not surprising that in any modern bookshop or indeed in any ancient library, the numbers of books on horror subjects far exceeds those speculating on utopias. Indeed writers of utopias are more likely to be considered naive, or at the best over hopeful. So often people will point to the bad things, the things that have gone wrong, the abuse of discoveries, but forget or purposely ignore the fact that for the large majority in the western world and in the major parts of the rest of the world the life we lead today is so, so, so every much more improved and humanised than that lived by our ancestors even a hundred years ago. And where has all those advances come from, all those things that today few people would want to be without, and even those that decide to live as Alternatives, still hold on to the essentials of modern live. We live in better houses, have running clean water, have heat and communications beyond anything our parents dreamt of. We have better medical treatment and health and age expectation than ever known on earth before and the means of enjoyment and relaxation have amplified beyond the wildest dreams of our ancestors. Nonetheless, this upside of human development, of the humanisation of homo sapiens, is the direct result of the advances made by scientists, and inventors. We cannot escape from the responsibility we have to those who from the earliest of times took the bold step of looking into the unknown, of doing something different to the majority of the group, of asking a new question, of trying out a new idea, of taking an unknown risk. We are today possessed with the idea of risk. Did the chap who first discovered fire burn his finger and shout, "no do not use fire it is dangerous and might kill you". Did some primitive clan sit around in their freezing cave, shivering in their scanty fur skins, debate the dangers of fire and decide it was too dangerous to use? If so, that tribe would have died out. Unfortunately today, inspite of the clear knowledge of the upside of scientific advances, there are those of influence and authority who would claim that enough is enough and that certain aspects of science should not be explored, that a moratorium is imposed on certain aspects so that new knowledge cannot be found. This view is based on the belief that once new knowledge is found, once a new technique is available that it will be used in ways that will either be dangerous or unethical. At present nowhere is this more evident than in the field of genetic engineering, especially with GM foods, with the fear of the future so obvious on so many lips. Whereas I have considerable sympathy with genuine concerns about safety and ethics, I have little respect for the anti-science culture that clutters their thinking, especially when their exponents live in and enjoy the *luxury* of modern life that is so immensely dependent upon scientific and medical advances. Surely, it is more likely as our human experience has shown so often before, that while Man often creates problems, we also solve them, as indeed otherwise the human race would have long since disappeared from the Earth.

The GM Controversy

But our concerns are nothing new and at the very launch of the genetic engineering era, in the mid 1970's, a great recombinant DNA debate raged across the world. This storm resulted from the famous Paul Berg's letter in 1974 when recombinant DNA procedures had just been worked out and it was felt by the scientists involved that certain experiments could carry unknown hazards. The scientists themselves, showing a great deal of humanity and unselfish concern, called for a moratorium on certain experiments and a great public debate ensued, analysing the whole question of hazards, ethics and practice. Never before has science been subjected to such scrutiny. In the UK, in 1975, Lord Ashby, chaired a working party, which resulted in the establishment of the Genetic Manipulation Advisory Group (GMAG). This group and its subsequent committees have played an important role over the years in clarifying and defining the procedures that should be used and also in separating the realities from the speculation and conjecture. Today, all work involving recombinant DNA requires approval of safety committees and is governed by well-defined codes of practice and working conditions. Although we must all be alert to new developments that may not be socially acceptable, and may contain 'potential risk', none of us,

117

scientists, politicians or indeed society as a whole, can escape the flow of the torrent, escape from the responsibilities that new discoveries provide. We cannot sit back and say No! - We will not stain our hands in studying the fundamentals of the atom because it may provide a means of a nuclear war. No! We will not study the silicon chip because it could lead to Big Brother watching us. No! We will not read the dictionary of genetics because some Frankenstein may lurk in the shadows of the distant future. Surely today more than ever before scientists must be more than logs merely adrift on the river. Rather, our logs must be upright, to stand strong and firm against the gathering clouds of stagnation, and retraction, that social attitudes and economic factors bear upon us. Now it is more essential than ever that scientists participate in how their work is exploited, and that they strive together with politicians and industrialists, medicals and agriculturalists to ensure that the application is always towards the common good. As all practicing scientists know, there is already a world wide unwritten code of practice of how science should be done and what is needed is an international agreement about how science should be exploited, although in reality, such an aspiration will be a long time in coming. Unfortunately, the current demands of wealth creation, being a high if not the top priority of funding science, has resulted in blurring of the distinction between fundamental science and technology in both the minds of politicians and the general public, resulting in the emergence of an anti science trend which should be of great concern to the future of society.

But it would be wrong for me to leave you with the feeling that everything is rosy; that there are no problems and the application of the new revolution in biology will lead to a Utopia. This indeed would be hoodwinking you in the most blatant way. There is no doubt that recombinant DNA procedures will present society with difficult and challenging problems that will require an immense amount of tact and a great deal of humanity to resolve. But into what new land of milk and honey shall we walk? What will a complete reading of the genetic dictionary of man reveal? Will it tell us why people take disease, who are more susceptible to cancer, what makes a good sportsman, a mathematician or an artist? Should this prove to be the case, I would fear, that in generations to come, it may be but a small step from the use of precise genetic screening probes for detection of well established and documented genetic defects or latent viral infections, on crucially important and highly acceptable medical grounds, to the use of genetic screening for pre-employment and other nonmedical but social, economic and educational reasons. To cure a young child from a genetic predisposition to suffer from smog or to assess whether a person is suitable for work in a hayfield or coal mine may become socially acceptable. Society may demand the correction of such so-called defects rather than attack the real problem of our environment and working conditions. It may be cheaper to do so, insurance companies may ask for it, employers may require it, future parents may desire it.

How the various political, social and economic systems throughout the world, that create public demand, convention and acceptability will manipulate this Genetic Literature is a major problem of the future that must be resolved on an international basis if mankind is not to fragment into genetically elitist groups. This will be the great dilemma of the future, the solution of which will require the utmost mutual respect and understanding, not only between the TWO CULTURES but also among ALL CULTURES.

So the river of gene biochemistry has come tumbling down this rocky glen into the oceans. What the future holds in store can be mere speculation - could Columbus have imagined the America of today or Mendel the split gene? Today the horizon is misty; the tide is on the turn. We sail forward into the Gene Age. A new language is upon us, irreversibly influencing our thoughts, our way of life, our morals and ethics, creating new social pressures as well as providing great benefits.

During the 1970's mankind donned a new pair of genes and took the first timorous steps into this new age. Where we go now is in the hands of the young generation that are blossoming forth from colleges and universities across the globe. I would ask them, nay, I would beg them, please, treat these new pair of genes with respect, tread in them with caution, and most important of all, walk in them with humility, remembering always, that the gene language is not of man's making.

A New Pair of Genes. Based on a lecture given by the author to Queen University, Belfast in 1980. Updated and modified in parts in 2000.